Jack Harvey
Breakthrough

~

JAMES HEWLETT

Content compiled for publication by Richard
Mayers of Burton Mayers Books.

Accies logo, icons and kit design by
Anthony Barbapiccola.
Cover by Martellia Design.

First published by Burton Mayers Books 2023

ISBN: 978-1-7396309-9-7

Typeset in Palatino Linotype

This is a work of fiction. Names, characters,
places, and incidents either are the product of
the author's imagination or are used fictitiously.
Any resemblance to actual persons, living or
dead, events, or locales is entirely coincidental.

www.BurtonMayersBooks.com

For Harvey and Robyn

Dream big. Always believe in yourself.

Love Dad

ACKNOWLEDGMENTS

One day I woke up, and just started writing. Writing I have discovered is a solitary world. Finding the inspiration to start, and then getting it out to you all is very much a team game!

This book was a dream of mine, but without the help of a whole host of people it would have remained just that, a dream.

I can't name everyone who helped, guided and inspired me along the way as it would just not be possible to fit their names all on these pages, but to all those who played a part, however small, I am truly grateful for all that you've done.

To Elizabeth, my better half – a talented writer in your own right. I knew if I could get you interested in a story about a footballer, I was onto something good! Your help, support and unwavering belief in me when things were getting tricky was invaluable.

Family is all important. We are there for each other no matter what: Mum, Andrew, Ruth and Peter, you've always had my back. This book is as much for you as it is for me.

To Lisa and students of Mont Nicolle School. You got the sneak preview of the very first draft. Thank you for your feedback that gave me the confidence to keep going.

To Richard and Burton Mayers Books, my publishers, you took a chance on my dream and helped me turn it into a reality. I hope that this is indeed the first of many Jack Harvey books and we will work together for many years to come.

Harvey and Robyn, this book is for you. This is to show you that anything truly is possible in this life if you really want it enough and are ready and prepared to just go for it.

Finally, the reader of this book. I hope to have inspired you, even a tiny bit to go out and live your dreams. Make them a reality. Be proud, don't give up. Dream big.

"IT'S HARD TO BEAT SOMEONE WHO NEVER QUITS." (JACK)

THWACK...!

The ball had skidded across the wet grass and smacked into the left-hand post.

40,000 groans from the crowd – so close.

It was 1-1 in the last game of the season. Accies (Academicals) had to win their final match to stay in the Premier division. The noise from the South End stand where the most passionate fans sat were chanting 'A-KEYS, A-KEYS, A-KEYS' in an attempt to lift their team.

The team that had won the League Championship only a few seasons ago, and were once regular challengers in the Champions League, had fallen on some tough times. The team had grown old, and the manager hadn't replaced his star players who struggled against the younger, fitter, and quicker sides.

I'm Jack Harvey, striker! I play for the best

team in the world – or at least we used to be one of them. When I first signed as a youth player, we fought for the biggest and best prizes in Europe. Now it was a darker time for the club: we were at the wrong end of the division and heading in only one direction. But we still had a chance to save ourselves.

I sat in the stands with my mate, Lucas. We had been best mates for as long as we could both remember. We lived on the same street, in a lovely (usually) quiet area of the town, about a mile from the ground. My house was small, but enough room for me, my mum and dad, and my football-mad sister Isabelle (or Izzy). We always had a lot of fun together. The chat between dad and I was almost always about the footie, mostly the Accies. I knew everything there was to know about the club. It was my passion. On match days when we were too young to go, we could hear the roar and the song from the stadium. It was electrifying and inspiring. We would kick a football in the yard for hours pretending we were the players driving the Accies to glory. I'd be the striker, Lucas would be in goal. We would go up to the local playing fields, both diving around until our knees had been stained green by the grass. Fast-forward 10 years: we were members of the academy, and under-18 youth team players for the Academicals, even though we were both just 16 years old.

'I can't believe this,' I exclaimed as I turned to face Lucas. 'There's five minutes to go, we HAVE to win.'

The yellow and blue wall of colour and noise behind us suddenly erupted, as, in a last throw of the dice, 36-year-old Dexter Brooks (or Dex as he was known), was coming on. The former England international had scored a record 268 goals for the club, plus 34 for England, including winning the Golden Boot in the 2006 World Cup. The crowd loved him, he always gave his best, but only five goals this season told its own story. He and the team were too old, too slow and needed a huge change. But for now, they just needed one goal, one more chance for the ball to land at his lethal boots to save their, and our, season. The crowd noise was deafening, and Lucas and I sang our hearts out. The rest of the youth team sat around us with other club officials and the players who weren't in the team, hands in the air, waving scarves, pennants, anything yellow or blue. It was an amazing sight and one that gave Accies the reputation of having the best fans in the League, if not the whole of Europe.

Only two minutes to go. It was all one-way now. Accies were pushing harder and pressing higher than ever. It was probably our best performance of the season. Superstar Portuguese forward Thiago Felipe whipped in a cross. It was headed clear, but only to Dex who hit it first time with venom in his boots. The crowd held its breath – then we let out another collective groan, heads falling into hands, as the ball clipped the crossbar and finished in the stands.

Now we were into injury time. We couldn't go down, it couldn't happen. It didn't seem possible as just a few weeks ago we seemed to be clear of relegation, but a dramatic change of form and ridiculous run of injuries to key players had resulted in ten defeats in a row. And with Broughton Albion picking up 16 points from their last six matches to sneak to within a single point, it was all down to these last few seconds. It was a huge turnaround, and now the Accies' future was hanging by a thread. One goal, one win would be enough, Broughton were winning their last game comfortably, but we knew it was still in our hands.

Whilst it had been a shocking season for the first team, for me it was the first season that I actually believed I might have a chance as a professional footballer. Lucas and I had been Accies Juniors, (the famous AXE academy) since we were both 11. We had played every under-18 game so far this season, and I thought we had done well. It helped that Lucas, as a goalkeeper, had been brilliant. We knew if we could get one goal, we wouldn't lose often. I had scored 27 goals in just 20 games, including three hat-tricks, my best academy season so far. However, we all felt that we were still a long way from the first team and playing in the Premier League. And unless a miracle happened in the next 120 seconds, that dream would be even further away than ever.

Deep into injury time, the Accies had thrown everyone forward except the keeper, but even he was on the halfway line. The ball was launched into the box, headed clear, Dexter leapt the highest of two defenders and headed it back where it fell awkwardly to J-D (Axel Juan-David) whose shot bobbled off the wet grass and into the grateful gloves of the goalkeeper.

And that was it. The referee gave a long blast on the whistle, which signaled the end, not only of the match but also of Accies' 54-year stay in the top division. The players slumped on the pitch, some in tears. The fans, distraught, did their best to try and sing, but the words would not come. I couldn't believe it. Right until the end, I believed we were going to get the goal we needed to stay up. I had not imagined the Accies being relegated, down into the Championship, the Second Division? That was crazy. We had won the top division 23 times and been successful in Europe, winning the old European Cup three times. But now we were down. It would be a long summer.

'Jack,' said Lucas sadly, 'what do you think will happen to us? Do you think we have a future here? Do you think they will keep us?'

'I don't know.' I admitted, 'Maybe not.'

I felt a hand on my shoulder. It was old Billy. No one really knew what Billy did at the club. With his wrinkled face and bright white hair (what was left of it) he looked about 100 years old and probably was, but he could still strike a football better than most of our current professionals. We all thought he must be a scout, or maybe even some kind of caretaker. He had played for the club decades ago and stayed on ever since. Everyone respected him, not just because he held the record for most first team appearances, (nearly 700!). He had a reputation of being a bit scary, especially when he found a pair of stray or misplaced boots in his pristine corridors. He had seen it all, done it all, and won nearly every club trophy there was to win.

'Jack me-lad,' he said, 'you and big Lucas just keep working hard, keep your heads down over the summer. You are the future of this club. You will bring it back to greatness, but you must believe in yourself.' He gave me a big broad smile, showing all the gaps left from teeth knocked out decades ago when he played the game.

'Remember,' he added, 'it's not about how you got knocked down, it's about how quickly you get back up again. I'll see you for pre-season, don't let me down.' Then he headed for the exit.

I turned to Lucas, gobsmacked. 'Did you hear that? Billy spoke to us! He knew our names! He knows who we are!'

'I know.' said Lucas with a huge grin,

In the gloom of relegation suddenly there was a ray of hope.

'Lucas, I'm only 16, do you really think we have a chance?'

'We will be nearly 17 by the time the season kicks off, well 16 and a half anyway,' Lucas replied hopefully, 'who knows.'

We walked out of the stadium side by side and began to jog, faster and faster until I gave it all I had and sprinted the last 500 metres leaving a puffing Lucas behind.

'With … that … pace,' he gasped, taking in a huge breath, 'you will … always have … a chance!'

"THE ONLY REAL MISTAKE, IS THE MISTAKE FROM WHICH WE LEARN NOTHING." (BILLY)

The season would begin for Lucas and me in early July, although we hadn't stopped training since the final day of the previous season. Billy's words were still stuck in our heads as we ran further, faster, and harder than we had ever run before. As a result, when the first proper pre-season training session came around, we were the fittest players in the academy by a mile.

One of the biggest changes the Accies' manager, Walter Rolland, had made in his time at the club, was to bring the academy and the first team all into one place to train. We ate in the same canteen, used the same pitches, and saw the best players close up every day. It was Walter's belief that when a good youngster was ready, it would be easier for him to join in training with the first team having already had some interaction socially. On the odd occasion, the academy players were tasked to be the opposition and mimic the team that the first team were due to play. I used to watch in awe of all the talent that Accies had on view, but now I was desperate to be a part of it. Up until very recently, we had such a good team. It was hard for the young players to break into the side. Most went out on loan and rarely came back. Only midfielder Jamie Curry had managed to keep a regular place in the first team squad in the last few years.

Walter Rolland was 'Mr Academicals'. He lived and breathed the club having been a player first, then a coach and finally a manager. He had overseen the first team for 15 seasons and had won every club trophy there was to win. The town and the club were at the very top of English football.

It would not last. The club had been sold five years ago to a ruthless businessman who refused to invest in the team. Walter had worked miracles to keep the club competitive and hang onto some great players despite the lack of funds. It was believed that on occasion he had paid hotel bills and sometimes covered the rent for some of the younger players out of his own money, just to keep them at the club.

Everyone loved him. He was a living, breathing, legend. But even he was now feeling the strain, and the results suffered.

Lucas and I stood on the side of our pitch watching the first team squad. It looked smaller, much smaller than ever before. We had noticed gaps in the players' car park when we arrived, and there were rumours everywhere of players leaving. The sports news channels were calling it a 'fire-sale.' Our best players were getting picked off by other Premiership and big European clubs, who had the promise of European football that they now would not get here. The club, having lost huge amounts of money because of relegation to the Championship, had no choice but to sell, and some refused to play in a division below where they thought they belonged. First out the door was German international, Stefan Adler, and then the Welsh brothers, Owen and Brent Davies, returned to their previous club.

In a huge shock, arch-rivals and one of the biggest sides on the planet, Liverton, pinched arguably our best player and captain, Matteo Samuel. Born in England to Italian parents, and son of the great Lorenzo Samuel who scored the winning goal in the 1982 World Cup, Samuel had played more games than any other current player for the Accies, over 400 in a ten year spell. The rumours were that he had a heated argument with Walter after our final game, and had refused to come to a pre-season training camp. Walter, who was known for being loyal, but ruthless, transfer listed him. But it was a massive blow when he actually went, even more so moving to our bitter rivals.

Pre-season was usually an exciting time of year, new players arriving always excited me, but this time it was not about who we would be signing, but who would be leaving. It was tough to take. The heart was being ripped out of the side. I sat with Lucas and the academy coach, Deiter Dedrich, after training.

'Lads,' Deiter declared, 'get your chins off the floor. This is a bad time for the club but for you it's an opportunity, you are head and shoulders above the other boys here. You are fitter and faster than most of the first team, be ready, Walt will come calling and you need to be ready, just in case.'

At 16 years, 198 days old, I knew I was still very young. I was younger than any other player to have played first team football in the history of the club, but after the sale of Samuel, another striker, it left the club with only two forwards – Dexter Brooks (now 37), and

Portuguese star Thiago Felipe, last season's top scorer, who with 22 goals, 16 in the Premier League, was about the only bright spot of the previous season. The club had somehow tied him into a long-term contract as they knew that without him we stood no chance of promotion.

At that moment I caught the eye of Josh Davies, the first team coach. He was waving me over, so I jogged round the side of the pitch to his dugout.

'Jack, we've been watching you in pre-season, we've been impressed. Walter wants to take you to York Town for the first game of the season as a substitute, you ok with that?'

I opened my mouth but no words came out, I just nodded.

'Good,' he said, 'go get your stuff and join in with the first team, tell Lucas too, Jurgen needs a break in goal and they want to do some corner routines and shooting practice.'

Jurgen Heinrich was a big lump of a goalkeeper, shorter than most and a bit tubby around the middle. But his agility was incredible. He had been a regular in the German national squad since he was 18 years old, winning nearly 50 caps. However, in the last couple of seasons his form, like the rest of the squad's, had dipped.

I couldn't believe it, training with the first team, I wanted to tell my mum and dad but there was no time,

'Lucas! LUCAS! Grab your gloves, Walter Rolland needs us, come on!'

We both sprinted over nearly clattering into six foot four inches of a human Scottish wall. Harry MacRendal was the most fearsome looking player I had ever seen – up close he was terrifying. Short hair and a grizzly reddish beard, with forearms that should be attached to a rugby player or a wrestler, not a footballer. Harry, or 'Mac' as he was known, had played over 100 times for Scotland, captaining them since he was 22.

'WOAH there lads, where's the emergency?' he said in his thick Scottish accent.

'Mr, Mr, er, um, Mr Rolland said he wanted us,' I blabbered.

'Well, go grab a ball and get in the line. Show us why he wants you. The big fella better be ready,' he said nodding at Lucas, who was already in goal bouncing around, hopping from one foot to another.

I knew Lucas was nervous, I was terrified. I closed my eyes and opened them to applause, Lucas had just turned a Thiago pile driver over the crossbar

'What a save lad, what's his name?' asked Mac.

'It's Lucas.' I replied, 'Lucas Cain.'

'Well, Jurgen Heinrich is in trouble if your mate Lucas Cain keeps playing like that.'

I smiled inside. I knew Lucas' nerves would be gone now.

My turn. *'This is it,'* I said to myself, *'this is what you've wanted all your life. It's simple, ping the ball into the coach, collect the return and smash it home. You've done this a million times.'*

My pass to Josh was perfect, but my first touch was a little loose as I tried to re-take his lay-off, and as I stretched, the ball ballooned up and over the bar.

'AGAIN JACK,' shouted Walter. 'Do it AGAIN. Hit the target lad – FOCUS.'

I felt humiliated as I joined the back of the queue. Then I felt this presence looming over me. It was Mac.

'You wouldn't be here if you weren't good enough youngster. Now focus. Do what you do, and do it with a smile on your face. You've done the difficult bit, you've been noticed. Walter already knows your name, OK?'

It was hard to disagree with him, he was enormous – most people agreed with him even if they didn't want to! The second time up, the pass was good, my first touch better, and as I struck the ball it arrowed to the top corner, screaming past Lucas who had no chance.

'Top bins lad,' Mac shouted as I jogged back.

I could see Walter scribbling something down. It felt great.

For the rest of the week, we both trained with the first team. Deiter was right, we were fitter and faster than each and every one of the first team, first in the sprints, first in the longer runs, it was just the strength I was lacking. I did my best but I would get bullied off the ball by both Mac and his new defensive partner, Henry George. George became our only major signing of the transfer window, coming in from Park Lane United who had also been relegated from the Premier League. As nice as it was to get him in (he was a funny and chatty guy), we all felt a little sad that so many of last season's team had left and not been replaced.

I felt great that evening as I devoured a massive bowl of pasta, but the message that pinged up on my phone came as a shock. Ever since we had joined in with the first team training we had been added to the messaging group. It was mainly news about players leaving, or training times and venues, but this one was different. In big, bold lettering the top of the message read:

ACCIES TEAM Verses York Town, Saturday afternoon. 3 pm KO

GK Jurgen Heinrich
RB Alfie Shepherd
LB Arlo Bernard
CB Harry MacRendal
CB Henry George
DM Axel Juan-David
LM Wyn Thomas
CM Jamie Curry
RM Sem Luuk
AM Thiago Felipe
F Dexter Brooks

Substitutes
Lucas Cain (GK)
Gianfranco Spaletti
Antony Joseph
Jeremy Klyne
Finlay Crane
Santiago Martin

And there, right there, at the end of the message…

Jack Harvey… MY NAME!

I'd made it? I HAD MADE IT!

'I'm in the first team squad! MUM, DAD, IZZY, Look at this! I'm in, I'm in! Woooo-hoooo!' I screamed.

We all bounced around the living room hugging, screaming and shouting.

"IT IS EASY TO SUPPORT SOMEONE
WHEN THEY ARE WINNING. THAT
TAKES NO COURAGE. TO STAND
BEHIND YOU WHEN THEY ARE
DOWN, AND WHEN YOU REALLY
NEED THEM, THAT TAKES
COURAGE." (DAD)

It was finally game day. It had felt like pre-season training had gone on forever. There were high hopes for the Accies in this new season. Despite our relegation, and eventually losing seven of the first team players who had played a significant role in recent seasons, most neutrals predicted an immediate return to the Premier League.

As I pulled on my kit, the nerves bubbled up. My hands trembled as I tried to tie my laces. It took me four attempts to tie one boot.

'Jack, take a big deep breath lad,' Walter said reassuringly. 'You're only a substitute. I know it's a big deal for you but just enjoy the experience. I'll only bring you on right at the end when we are winning and things are going well, ok?'

It didn't help. Eventually, after tying my second boot in a double knot, I ran to the toilet and was horribly sick.

'Feel better?' It was Mac.

In my eyes, he was still the scariest man on planet earth! He had been brilliant with me since that first day's training. He was fearsome, but as I had discovered, if you try hard, and do your best, he will look after you – and definitely don't try and put the ball between his legs! I had nut-megged him earlier in the week in training, and when I came to get dressed after my shower I found that he had stolen my shoelaces and filled my socks and trainers with shower gel and flour!

'All ok pal?' He had asked with a big grin on his face when I discovered the prank. I glared at him angrily, but my mood softened as I heard the giggles of the other players.

'Ah you've been done kiddo' said Jamie Curry. 'In my first week he hid my shorts, I had to train in underwear for the whole of that day!'

'Yes Mac, of course,' I replied to the giant Scotsman, I gave him a half-grin as I slip-slopped, out of the dressing room and into the carpark with my soggy socks sticking out of my lace-less trainers!

Five minutes to kick-off, I looked in the mirror. I looked as green as if I had been on a tiny boat in the middle of a massive storm.

'It will pass,' Mac said, 'don't worry. We will score three or four then you can come on and bang in your first goal. Ok?'

I did my best to force a smile.

Walking out with the team and into the lion's den made me feel ten feet tall. I was so proud. I had seen my sister Izzy earlier, all kitted out in an Accies strip, plus her scarf, banner and hat she wore every time she watched me play. She was a fanatical Accies supporter like I was, and rarely missed a game home or away if dad let her, so it felt good knowing she was sat in the stands. As the captain of the ladies' under-16's, she was also a huge talent, and the fittest and fastest human I had ever come across. She would be as desperate to watch me come on as I was to get on!

Our first match in the Championship was away to a middle-of-the-table side, York Town. No one expected them to get promoted, or to go down either. They were happy where they were. Their fans understood this and knew that hosting the fallen giants of Accies was like a cup final for them. By kick-off, the noise had reached levels I had never heard outside of our stadium, except this time every kick we made was booed, and each tackle they made was roared on like they had won the World Cup.

'Lucas, LUCAS,' I shouted, 'this is crazy, huh!'

'I know. Is this what it's going to be like every game?' he asked.

'I reckon so, every team will want to beat us. We are the Accies after all.'

The crowd roared again, the York Town winger had robbed Arlo at full back and raced down the line, he whipped in a lovely cross right onto their striker's head and the net bulged. 1-0 York Town!

'No!' I shouted. This wasn't meant to happen.

It got worse, right on half time Alfie Shepherd picked up a second yellow card for a deliberate handball and was sent off. From the free kick, they went two up. The ball, driven hard and low, smacked into the shins of Mac, and bobbled into the opposite corner, leaving Jurgen Heinrich hopelessly wrong-footed in the Accies goal.

At half time the players looked shell-shocked. A few of them had clearly thought this would be an easy three points, and now we were 2-0 and a man down. Walter Rolland wrote furiously on the whiteboard, rearranging the team, telling us we were better than what we had shown. He remained calm, Mac did not. Mac paced up and down the dressing room with a face like thunder. J-D and Wyn Thomas were shouting at each other – each blaming the other for the goals conceded. I looked at Lucas, he looked at me. We daren't say a word.

The second half was better, but York Town knew they could just play the ball about and make us run. The team tried, but with two goals to peg back it was not to be. Time ran out and I remained on the bench. It was a big disappointment not to get on, but also a relief. Our forwards had been kicked black and blue by the opposition. Dexter could hardly walk and Thiago looked shell-shocked. It wasn't like this last season in the Premier League. In the Championship, whilst the defenders weren't as good, they seemed stronger and very physical. Some of the tackling was very tough, but the referee was happy to let the game carry on.

There would be a lot of sore and bruised players the next day. Walter Rolland was not happy with the referee, but even less happy with the players.

As tough as it was, the squad responded well in training. That week we quickly shook off the shock of the defeat, and by Wednesday we had begun laughing and joking in training again. That defeat? It was a one-off, surely.

'We knew it was tough in this League,' barked Walter, 'now you know just how tough. We won't make the same mistakes again.'

Our first home match against Sanford Warriors, again should have been a straightforward three-pointer, but we fared a little better than last week. It wasn't the packed stadium we were used to, but our home support at the 'kop end' was as good as it always was. We huffed and puffed, and they defended well, closing down the space and restricting our chances to long-range shots and half chances. There were only about five minutes left, with the game still at 0-0, when the Sanford winger miss-hit a horrible cross that looped high towards our goal, Jurgen backpedalled as fast as he could but the ball was over him, brushing the post as it dropped in. 0-1, what a fluke. There was not enough time to get back at them and the game finished in a second shock defeat.

We had lost our first two games, and when

the third ended 0-0, it was obvious where the issues lay: we just could not score goals. To add to the dark mood that was closing in around the team, last season's top scorer, Thiago, had picked up a leg injury that needed a minor operation. But it meant that he would miss at least the next six weeks of the season.

In Thiago's absence, the team continued to struggle, although our first goals did eventually come. Dexter opened our account for a 1-1 draw in our second home match, which was quickly followed by a pulsating 2-3 defeat – both goals from the frustrating Italian Gianfranco Spaletti. 'Franco' on his day could challenge the best players in the world, but he was so lazy. He was known as a 'luxury' player, someone who was great when playing well, but when things did not go his way, he was nowhere to be found. We all knew this, but Walter knew that when he played, he could beat any team almost on his own. It was just that he didn't do it very often.

We did at least begin to show fight as a team. We had been 3-0 down after a poor first half, but we came back well after the introduction of Spanish player Santiago Martin and were a post width away from equalising. The team was low on confidence, lacking inspiration. Walter seemed to be holding it all together, but away from the media spotlight, he looked broken and downhearted.

Seven games into the season, the Accies, a team that everyone expected to get promotion easily, had a record of won none, drawn two, and lost five, including a humiliating 0-3 away defeat to tiny Wealdmore Falcons. We had scored only five and had conceded 14. We were bottom of the table, and a massive 19 points behind the top two teams already.

The news reports suggested that defeat in the next game against top-of-the-table Western Villa would be the end for Walter Rolland. The team had to win, but still having not made my debut, there was not much I felt I could do to help.

The night before the game, I was lying on the sofa chatting to my parents and playing a card game with Izzy, when the doorbell rang. It was Walter.

'Good evening Mr. and Mrs. Harvey, hope you are well. I was just bringing you some spare tickets for tomorrow's game, I hope you will be there?'

We all looked confused.

'Jack, I know you've not had a chance yet, but with Thiago missing we need someone who can score us some goals, and with your pace, I think this will be the perfect game for you to make your debut.'

'You're, you're bringing me on tomorrow?' I spluttered.

'No, Jack. I am starting you. It's your time. We need a win and I have nothing to lose. I'm sure you have heard the reports, it's true. We lose tomorrow and I will almost certainly be sacked. I just want you to go out there and have some fun. Win or lose, I want to be the manager who gave Jack Harvey his first team debut. You, young man, if you work hard, could go all the way, make this team great again.'

'I won't let you down sir,' I said, standing to attention.

'I know you won't,' he replied, with the biggest smile as he left.

Then came an ear-splitting POP! from the kitchen and dad ran in with a bottle of champagne, foaming bubbles flowing over the top.

'I knew you could do it son, I knew it. I bought this bottle the day you signed your first schoolboy contract. Now we will celebrate, but you can't drink any. You have goals to score tomorrow!'

'I'm so proud of you bro.' Izzy hugged me so hard I thought my ribs would break. 'You are going to be amazing.'

I lay in bed that night, my head swimming with my thoughts about what could happen tomorrow. Even though we were not allowed to tell anyone team news before the game I had texted Lucas. He was delighted.

'You will be amazing,' his message said. *'You are already the best striker the club has, everyone is saying that. You'll be brilliant, I know it.'*

I was still awake when my phone rang again. It was Mac.

'Still awake lad? Walt told me the news. How do you feel?'

'To be honest Mac', I replied, 'I'm terrified, what if we lose? Then Walter gets sacked, I won't get another chance.'

'Don't worry,' Mac said. 'We will all look after you, tomorrow is your day. Walt will still be the manager next week. We ARE going to win and you WILL score. Trust me. Now go to sleep! Goodnight superstar.'

Before I could reply, he had hung up. I laughed to myself, despite the obvious scariness, I really liked Mac, although if I got a goal bonus, I might have to buy myself a few more pairs of socks!

"DREAMS CAN COME TRUE WHEN WE HAVE THE COURAGE AND DESIRE TO PURSUE THEM." (MUM)

I'd woken up buzzing. It was now 6AM and I had been up and about since 4AM. I was beside myself with butterflies. I'd fiddled with games on my computer, not really concentrating. I'd made my bed, got back in it, made it a second time, then tidied my bedside table – which I had then realised I hadn't cleaned for a while, so I did that too.

I'd folded and repacked my entire t-shirt drawer and rearranged my match card collection into teams and position order. Anything to distract myself from what was to come. I was still so nervous.

I checked my phone; it was full of messages from the team. They had all been given the heads up. My favourite one was from Dex.

'My record is only 268 goals. Let's see what

you can do today!'

'Morning superstar,' it was my dad, unshaven, fuzzy hair and still in his baggy PJ's. 'How long you been up?' he asked as he came into my room with a big cup of tea. The faded old cup read, 'The Accies, European champions 1998'. It was my dad's favourite cup; no one was allowed to drink out of that cup. I felt honoured.

'Not long dad,' I fibbed. 'Just woken up now. I'm just so excited for the game today. I can't believe I'm starting, my debut, and against Western Villa, it's amazing!'

'Incredible' he said, 'but you've earned it. You've worked your socks off. This team can't score goals and you can. With your pace, those Villa players will have no chance.'

'I hope so,' I thought. Western had a reputation of being tough at the back. They had a solid defence and usually played with three central defenders who loved a physical battle. Basically, that meant unless I could stay clear of them, they would try and kick me into the stands! Their two wingbacks were fast and ridiculously fit, but not as fast as me!

'Do you feel nervous?' my dad asked me.

'Yes, a bit', I said. 'Actually, yes. A lot. I'm terrified I won't be good enough'.

'Of course, you ARE good enough,' Dad

continued. 'You've always been good enough. You've been the best player in every team you've played in since you were five or six years old. It's ok to be nervous. It's ok to have that churning in your tummy. It shows you are ready.'

I felt better after that. I always did after a chat with dad. He always seemed to know what to say and when to say it. Praise when I had done well; guidance when I did not. He knew when I was down, and how to pick me up. He had seen me play in every game since I was six (except for when he was at work). He even used to come and watch me at training! I was so lucky.

I bounced down the stairs for my breakfast and grinned when I saw Izzy. She was sat at the table in her PJ's, Onesie and my Accies bobble-hat. She grinned back at me through a mouthful of toast. I realised I was ravenous, and wolfed down a big bowl of cereal, yoghurt and fruit, and my usual jam on toast with another huge mug of tea, this time made by my mum who had been fussing about all morning. I think she was nervous too, more than my dad who was just so happy!

I said goodbye to Izzy who was so excited to be coming to actually see me play.

'I'll shout the loudest Jack, I'll be the one to

cheer you on!' she shouted as I left. I set off down the road to meet Lucas to do our usual walk to the ground, to have the pre-match meeting and maybe a massage to help me warm up.

Before I had even walked six doors down the street, I had so many people wishing me luck.

'Good luck lad,' - A man in an Accies shirt I had never seen before was walking to the game with his two sons. The boys were smiling and giving me the thumbs up.

'Go get them today. We are all rooting for you.'

The best wishes carried on all the way to the ground. Somehow it had been leaked that I was starting, and news was spreading fast. Everyone had been shocked and surprised by the poor start we had made. Despite losing some of our best players, nobody had expected us to be this bad. The fans were desperate for some hope, for a win, and it appeared that they had put their hope in me!

As Lucas and I arrived at the ground, we saw the team room was nearly full. I was usually one of the first, but there was a different atmosphere today. The players were quieter, more focused than I had seen them. We all knew what would happen if we lost. Everyone loved Walter and it would be devastating to lose him, not just as a manager, but also as a person. He had been brilliant with me from day one. It was no surprise really that he had known my name. He had learnt the names of everyone in the club, from the cleaners and groundskeepers, to the academy players and kitchen staff. He insisted that we all did the same and treated everyone in the club like family, no matter whether what their role was. If they worked for Accies, then they were important. If The Accies was a family, then Walter Rolland was definitely the father figure.

Walter stood up, at the front of the coach as we set off.

'Ok lads, we all know what's at stake here today, but I want you to forget about my position and what might happen. Concentrate on the game, leave it all out there on the pitch and bring back the three points for them.' He pointed out of the windows to all the fans waving us off with their yellows and blues. 'They believe, now you need to believe as well. Believe in yourselves, believe in your team-mates. We all know young Mr. Harvey is getting his debut today; help him, guide him, but don't be scared to let him run, we know how fast he is, Western doesn't. One other change to the team, Jamie Curry has failed a fitness test, so Santi is in, and Monty is on the bench.'

The wonderfully named Watson Augustus Montgomery had joined us on loan from an American team earlier in the week. His father was a billionaire who built super-yachts for the super-super rich. Monty had decided not to follow in his father's footsteps and become a footballer instead, much to his father's disgust and disappointment. Monty didn't care. He had a dream and followed it with drive and determination. He was quiet off the pitch, but in training we had hit it off straight away, his pinpoint crossing had given me a hat-trick in our final practice run-out before the game. I was very happy he had made it, at least to the bench.

Arriving at the ground, it was all a sea of black and red, their fans were as hostile as their defence, banging on the side of the coach and letting off red flares as we drove past.

'Look youngster, look at them,' said Mac, 'I love this, I absolutely love this. This atmosphere is as close as an international, or to a big European game as you can get.'

Whilst I was a bit intimidated - in fact all the noise and the colour terrified me - Mac was getting even more excited. He seemed to grow bigger standing there, filling the coach gangway with his muscles and his beard. Whatever happened, I knew he had my back, and it was reassuring to see him grinning at the vast crowds of Villa supporters as they shouted not very nice things in our direction.

'They don't really mean it, Jack' he said. 'They just want to try and scare us. It never works on me. I love it. It fires me up and makes me play better. Bring it on!'

We got changed. The dressing room was much smaller than I was used to, with only one small toilet. The windows were wedged open, so we had to shout to drown out the noise of the home fans.

'Welcome to Western Villa, Jack,' said Josh, the first team coach. 'They try to have you beaten before you even set foot on the pitch. Don't let them scare you, it's 11 verses 11 and the grass is still green. Run your socks off and you won't go far wrong.'

My hands were trembling once again as I laced up my boots, then as I looked up, Walter reached over with an Accies shirt.

'A debut shirt young lad,' he smiled. 'You'll never forget today, whatever happens, whatever the score. Give your best. This is where dreams come true.'

He gave me my shirt, big bold letters across

the back, HARVEY with the number 16 underneath. Written in tiny lettering just above my name was the club motto in Latin, "Ad astra per aspera" which meant 'Through adversity to the stars'. Basically, it meant that the way to the top is often difficult and hard work. It filled me with pride to think that this was now mine.

'Thanks boss,' I said. 'I won't let you down.'

'I know you won't,' he replied with a smile as he turned to walk off to the dugouts.

Just as we were about to run out, I felt a big hand on my shoulder, it was Lucas.

'Mate, I'm so proud of you, whatever happens. We've been dreaming of this forever. Now go win it for us.'

Kick off!

Boom, a huge roar, the wall of noise hit me. Whilst we had struggled so far this season, we knew the Villa game was the biggest of our season. Historically we'd always had close battles on the pitch and, as our nearest neighbours this season, the rivalry between us and the Villains - (as we called them) – would be even more intense. Until they were relegated a few seasons ago, the games were always the highlight of the season. End to end, always with loads of goals. The fans had waited a long time to see this.

The first ten minutes passed in a blur, I hardly had a touch, and when I did, I quickly lost it. The Villa defenders were all over me. The good news was both Henry and Mac were having a storming game at the back for us. If I thought I had it hard, the Villa forwards had it doubly hard trying to get behind our two monster central defenders.

But as they say, good things never last; despite their defensive heroics, the luck seemed to desert us once again, as a fierce cross from the right clipped a Villa player who was not even looking, sending Jurgen the wrong way and in. 0-1. My shoulder slumped, I'd hardly had a kick and we were losing, again. I trudged off at half time expecting to get subbed.

Walter seemed surprisingly upbeat.

'Wyn, take a shower, Monty, you're on.'

Monty's face lit up, although he did well to avoid the glare of Wyn Thomas who was not amused at having to come off and take a half time shower. Wyn hadn't been that bad. He had worked hard, but we needed more help up front. We were defending too much and too deep.

'We are still in this game,' he said. 'Monty is going to help us change the pattern of play now, instead of passing to feet, put it behind their defenders, Jack's pace will do the rest.'

After all the bad games we had put in recently, it was strange to see Walter so positive, but his words seemed to work as the players heads visibly came up again, and we looked ready.

The second half was only seconds old when Monty skipped past a Villa player looked at me and clipped an amazing pass over my defender.

I spun past him, with no one but the keeper between me and the goal, when all of a sudden I was on the floor. The defender had clipped my heels and sent me tumbling. Mac was screaming for a red card, but it was just a yellow, AND a free kick in a dangerous position. Arlo was our usual free kick taker, but he could just as easily clear the top of the stand as score from them, so I just closed my eyes and crossed my fingers.

I needn't have feared, the free kick was one of his best, it dipped and swerved and was heading for the bottom corner until the keepers' desperate fingertips somehow clawed out and turned it onto the post, but Dexter was there to smash home the rebound. 1-1. Our bench erupted.

'Yes lads, come on, it's ours now, let's win this,' he shouted as he ran back to the centre with the ball under his arm. For the next ten minutes we attacked at every opportunity, balls over the top, left and right. Monty was hitting amazing passes across the pitch, and I could see the defender who was marking me was starting to puff quite hard.

'Monty,' I shouted, 'give me the ball.'

He fired in a pass a bit too high and hard, but I just about managed to get my toe on it, flicking the ball up and over the defenders' leg, who ended up on his bum. I knew I was clear, and this time no one was catching me. I raced towards the goal and at that moment everything seemed to slow down, I could hear our fans screaming 'go-oooooon,' the keeper came out, I glanced left to see if I could pass the ball but no one else was in sight. I looked down and put my laces through the ball as hard as I could. It ripped past the keeper before he could react, and the net bulged! 2-1

'YEEEEEEEEEEEEEAAAAAAAAAAAAAAA HHHHHHHHH'

My head exploded with joy as I ran around like a lunatic until Mac got hold of me.

'Told you,' he screamed over the noise, 'I told you that you would score. What a great goal, brilliant. Five minutes left. DON'T STOP RUNNING!'

And I didn't. I ran and ran, chasing every

ball. I chased down defenders, I closed down their keeper constantly. Every time the ball was near me, I sprinted like my life depended upon it. I didn't get another chance, but I made sure they didn't either, and our defenders happily mopped up anything that came in their direction.

The final whistle blew. Yes, we had won. FINALLY, we had won. I had scored the winner? I scored the winner!!!

'I don't think I could ever feel happier than this,' I said whilst receiving a bear hug from Walter. I could see the relief in his face. 'I can't believe it!'

'Me too' Walt said. 'Enjoy tonight, we've a lot more games coming up for you if you keep playing like that.'

Sitting next to Lucas on the coach for the short ride back home, I stared out of the window. The red and black army had long since disappeared, and now all we could see was blue and yellow fans singing and dancing as they made their way back home.

'You've done that, youngster,' said Mac. 'You've given them back hope, the pride of the city. They will all have a brilliant week because of you. I don't think I've ever seen someone run as far, as fast, or as hard as you did today, and in your first match!'

'Thanks Mac,' I said, and I closed my eyes. I daren't admit it, but I was exhausted and fell sound asleep in seconds.

"SUCCESS DOES NOT HAPPEN BY ACCIDENT. IT IS HARD WORK, LEARNING AND SACRIFICE, BUT MOST OF ALL, LOVING THE GAME YOU PLAY." (WALTER)

Training that week passed in a blur. Everyone greeted me with a smile, with pats on the back from the coaching team and big smiles from the canteen staff. My dad's phone ran red hot from all the journalists who wanted the big story. Who I was, where I came from, what was my favourite colour?

My dad had been asked to attend the offices of Walter Rolland. It was a bit odd, but we went with it. Dad arrived at the training ground the day before our next match against East Cove. Walter wanted a chat with both of us together. I was a bit nervous as I thought things had been going well in training especially after my goal-scoring debut.

'Morning Mr Harvey, come in Jack,' he said as we arrived at his office. Walter's office was an amazing bright room overlooking the training ground. In the background the magnificent Accies stadium loomed large. All over the walls were pictures of sporting greats; footballers, rugby players, elite athletes, the best of all sports. Motivational quotes from famous people were hung between each set of pictures. It was an amazing office, and I could see straight away why Walter was such an inspiring man.

'Gentleman, good morning,' Walter said again, 'I won't keep you long. As you know the club has had difficulties with its finances since the relegation. We are going to have to slowly see out some of the older players and bring in players like Jack to keep us going. I just want to assure you that the club sees Jack as the future, and we would like to offer him this.'

He pushed a stack of papers towards my dad, on the front page it read:

Professional Players Contract

Between Accies Football Club and Jack Harvey…

My eyes bulged!
'It's a five-year contract Jack,' Walter

continued. 'Take your time, read over it, have a think.'

'Do you have a pen?' I asked. I had already reached the back page where it said signature. Walter and my dad both burst out laughing. I had an enormous smile on my face. I was a proper player now, a professional footballer. They were actually going to pay me to play football. I couldn't believe what I was seeing.

'Go home, tell your mum,' Walter said, 'I'll see you here tomorrow bright and early for the East Cove game ok?'

'Yes boss! I'll be the first one here I promise,' I blurted out with excitement.

The champagne corks went off once again once we were back at home, the whole family - including Lucas and his parents - had come round. Lucas had been sat outside the office when we left, and his news was as astonishing as mine.

True to his word, Walter had been forced to sell some of the older more experienced players. Our goalkeeper Jurgen Heinrich had gone, back to Germany. He didn't want to play in a lower league and risk losing his place in the German national squad. After watching Lucas train and play in a few youth-team matches, Walter had allowed Jurgen to leave. Lucas was in for the

East Cove game tomorrow!

'That's amazing news mate, I'm so pleased for you,' I said to a beaming Lucas, as we sat and watched the others drinking the champagne. We had both refused a glass as we had a game the next day, and I thought champagne was disgusting anyway!

'Thanks Jack,' he said. 'Walter told me it didn't matter if I made a mistake, he said you'd just score more goals!'

We both chuckled. Lucas didn't really make mistakes, he was such a calm person; even if he did let in a goal, it never seemed to worry him.

'All the best goalkeepers in history let goals in mate,' he once told me. And he was right, his favourite phrase he kept repeating was: 'there's no point in dwelling on what you've just done, focus on what you can do now, what you can change to make it better next time. You can never stand still. The moment you stop and admire yourself and where you are, someone else will go past you.'

It was sound advice, and that thought was in my head after five minutes of the Cove match. I'd already had one amazing opportunity but had scuffed the floor and the ball had bobbled harmlessly into the arms of the smiling keeper.

'Not a chance little boy,' the keeper laughed

as he ran past to thump the ball clear.

My cheeks flushed with anger. Who did he think he was? I've just signed a five-year contract with one of the best teams in history.

Whatever he had said though, worked against me. The very next pass that came to me, I mis-controlled, and whilst lunging to get it back, I caught an East Cove player on the shin, who screamed as he fell to the floor. Suddenly, I was surrounded by Cove players, pushing and shouting. The referees whistle was blasting; long and loud. It wasn't until Mac came in and removed me that I could breathe. I thought that was it.

'You need to calm down son', the referee said. 'That was rash and dangerous. I have every right to send you off, but I'm going to give you a second chance. Yellow card!'

'Thank you, sir, sorry sir,' I said looking at the ground.

If I was intimidated by the referee and the Cove players, it was nothing to the look I got from Mac.

'Get your head right lad,' he shouted. 'You are better than that. Don't let them put you off, be stronger in your mind. They know you can beat them with your skill, so they are trying to slow you down in other ways.'

He stomped off back to his position for the free kick, which luckily was excellently claimed by Lucas. The crowd cheered their approval. They could already see the potential in this new look team. Two fresh new faces on the pitch, and the bench was also full of youngsters, now that a big chunk of the older senior faces from last season had been moved on.

One of those faces was a new kid we had signed from Old Wimbledonians, Zac Smith. Zac had signed, initially only on loan, but if we did go back up to the Premier League the deal was that he would sign permanently.

Zac was my type of player. There was no doubt he had talent. He could pass, shoot, tackle, the lot. But what made him stand out, even at 18 years old, was his work rate. He didn't stop, ever!

'Why run when you can sprint, get there faster, get the job done quicker, Jacky,' he said to me at his first training session. I liked him straight away and was hoping that Walter would put him in the team soon. Walter was loyal to his older players, but like Monty, once they got a chance, he just couldn't leave them out. I was hoping this would happen to Zac, and soon.

The game against Cove had reached half-time with no goals. Lucas had done well, made saves when he needed to, but again we struggled to break down the opposition defence. Walter made a few changes; Zac was now on for Jamie Curry. He still wasn't moving right after his injury, but he hadn't played well today either. The other change was a 19-year-old fellow Academy player, Irishman Finbar Talbot who came on for Gianfranco Spaletti. Spaletti was having one of his lazy days, and caught one of Walters fearsome glares as he threw his shirt to the floor in disgust. Fin, like Monty, was quick, agile and could see a pass quicker than anyone I knew. He was very quiet on and off the pitch, but as long as his boots did the talking, Walter was happy, and so was I.

And he did just that. Straight after the restart Zac thumped into the Cove captain, sending him sprawling, before finding Fin with a typically inch perfect pass. Fin played a quick one-two, and curled a lovely pass round the back of the last defender and without even breaking stride, I passed the ball into the bottom corner 1-0.

'YEEEEEEEEAAAAHHHH, GET IN!'

The crowd was bouncing, 'Oh Jackee Jackee,' they sang. I couldn't believe it. Two goals in two games!

Two became three soon after. This time Monty, after beating two or three Cove players, rolled the ball across the six-yard box and all I had to do, once again, was tap it into the empty net with the keeper sprawling.

When Dexter smashed a failed clearance into the top corner to make it 3-0, we all relaxed. Walter, who had the weight of the world on his shoulders just two weeks ago, was beaming. He had moved out half of his squad and replaced them with untried and untested kids, and we were all on fire.

Final score, three goals to nil. More importantly, we had the three points. We were finally heading up the table. We had a long way to go to catch the early-season pacesetters, but as I walked into the dressing room and looked around, all I could see was happy smiling faces.

We were going to do this.

"HARD WORK BEATS TALENT AND SKILL, WHEN TALENT AND SKILL DOESN'T WORK HARD." (IZZY)

The games were coming thick and fast now. Four games in two weeks would test the younger players' powers of recovery, but I was confident that we really did have what it takes. Walter took the heat off us in the media, so we could concentrate on training and playing.

'We have a long way to go,' he told the news stations. 'We have had a really poor few games and have given all our rivals a big head-start. We are now playing catch-up, but these young lads we have brought in just want to play football, and that's what we will do.'

And we did exactly that. 'Free Flowing Fun Football' was the headline in the local paper after the Newford Celtic game. We had won 4-1 away, Monty and Zac getting their first goals, with an Arlo penalty and Mac's towering header finishing them off. I had played particularly well without scoring, setting up the first two goals, and causing havoc against a usually secure defence.

We struggled to get going on a cold Wednesday night in the capital against promotion rivals Park Lane. But once Dexter had headed in a second-half corner, we were off and running, finishing 3-1 winners. Park Lane was one of the more fancied sides to get promotion, so to win, and convincingly, again playing away from home, was a brilliant result.

Back at the Accies stadium, I scored another brace of goals against Arlington, before hitting a late winner verses Oxfield the following week, which made me briefly the clubs' top scorer (before Dexter hit a hat-trick in the next match). At 37-years old, Dexter was clearly loving having a bit of extra space in the Championship division, compared to the 100mph all-action Premier League. And whilst he was coming to the end of his career, his input to me personally was incredible.

After no wins in seven matches, we had won the next seven on the bounce, scoring a magnificent 18 goals, with Lucas only conceding three. It was some turn around. We had been transformed from a beatable, weak, goal-shy team, to one that was exciting, aggressive, confident and goal-hungry.

The intense nature of our all-action game plan did begin to take its toll though. First, we lost Zac to a leg injury. Then Monty, after a bad challenge right at the end of the Wimbledonians match. We had thought he had broken his leg initially, but luckily it was just bad bruising. Dexter, at his age, was beginning to struggle to play every game, and needed a rest, and with Harry George suspended after collecting five yellow cards, it was a much-changed side that ran out against Manford Rovers. Like us, Manford were one of the game's great sides. European Royalty, they called themselves, having won the European Champions cup four times. They were on a similar downward path to us, after their billionaire owners had pulled out. It left the club in deep debt. They couldn't afford to keep their big stars, and they fell into the Championship a couple of years before we did. After a poor season last time out, this season they had regrouped, restructured and brought in some very clever signings. They were certainly back with a bang, currently four points clear of Western Villa at the top of the table and scoring goals for fun, double the amount we had already.

I was starting up front, virtually on my own. We were going to try and hit them with a counter-attack game. Suck them into our half, then once we had won the ball back, pounce hard and fast, using our strengths. But Manford had other ideas, and just didn't give us a sniff.

They dominated the ball everywhere, leaving us to chase shadows. It was no surprise to the neutrals really that they scored first. Fifteen minutes had passed when Antony Joseph, another of my academy pals, left a back pass horribly short, and the Manford winger was able to clip the ball past Lucas for 0-1. From their next attack they nearly scored again, this time Lucas - flying away to his left - palmed the ball over the bar for a corner. The crowd was on their feet. Lucas had made himself a hero almost as much as I had in our short time in the first team. Local boys playing their hearts out, and playing well, for a team they had supported all their lives; the fans loved it. But they didn't love what happened next. An-swinging corner was won by a Manford player, and his header, on target, hit Arlo's arm. The referee had no hesitation. Penalty. And a red card for poor Arlo!

Arlo was gutted, as he trudged off with tears in his eyes. It was a complete accident, but as it stopped them scoring, the referee had no choice but to send him off. And as the ball flew in for 0-2 you could see a few heads drop; the crowd had gone silent after a typically noisy start. With just 20 minutes of the game gone, we were two nil down with only ten players.

They battered us after that. I hardly had a kick. I was running in circles getting more and more frustrated. Somehow, we made it to half time without conceding another, but even though Walter told us we were still in it, I could see we'd already lost. My head was down, and after Manford scored again to make it 0-3 after an hour of the game, and having picked up a silly yellow card for kicking the ball away in frustration, I was taken off. I'd hardly had a touch in the second half, and I deserved to be hooked. It still hurt though. I tried to watch the rest of the match, but watching Lucas pick the ball out of his net twice more was too much to take.

The away fans were singing 'champions' and 'we're gonna win the league' quite clearly trying to wind up and annoy our fans, well at least those who had bothered to stay. The stands were emptying long before the final whistle, which couldn't come soon enough. We'd come down after our fantastic run with a bump. All the earlier optimism had been sucked out of us, booing at the final whistle was something you did not hear from the Accies supporters, but we had deserved it. Whist we did not play well, our fans could usually accept that, but we stopped trying. We let them have the ball and didn't fight hard enough. We deserved nothing from the game and fully deserved the criticism we received from the stands.

The dressing room was a desperate sight. A mixture of sadness, embarrassment and anger. Some of the players refused to say a thing. Some couldn't say enough, loudly. Walter didn't say a thing. He didn't need to. We knew we had let everyone down. The journey home was awful, and even though it took a little under 10 minutes, I felt every eye on me, and every step felt slow and difficult, like I was stepping in wet cement.

The fallout from the Manford game was extreme. We were slated. The red card for Arlo was harsh, but in truth we were very poor, and losing a player did not change the way the game was going. I think we would have lost heavily anyway, even with all eleven players on the pitch. After all the good press I had received, I was also criticised heavily. It was not nice, and in training that week I was rubbish. I couldn't shoot straight, I over-hit every pass, lost every tackle and was slow to react to everything. Mac had serious words with me.

'Listen Jack, you need to sort yourself out,' he said. 'It's just one game. We were all rubbish, not just you. Every time from now on you get praised remember this moment, and every time you get bad stuff said about you, you can remember all the goals you have scored.'

He was right of course. It was just one bad performance in an otherwise great start to my professional career. I had been brilliant, so there was always going to be a game when things didn't go well. I just wasn't quite ready for the headlines in the papers saying I was too young, and that Walter should not have started me in that game as I wasn't experienced enough.

We again struggled to get going against Landon Borough in the next game, at least saving a draw this time. Fin scoring his first for the club, a lovely goal, beating two players before curling a beautiful shot into the bottom corner.

I had been dropped for the Borough game. I couldn't complain, my attitude sucked. Walter had hauled me into his office once already that week and today he had given me a proper dressing down.

'Jack my lad, the Manford game, that's a lesson for you right there, probably the most valuable one of the season. We keep going, we keep trying, no matter what. No matter how hard it is, or how desperate the situation: you never give up. Ever. Anything could have happened. But we will never know. Go home. Sulk if you need to, get over it. Come back Monday morning and train harder than ever. Win back your place in this team.'

As always, Walter was right, and I did train hard. Walter wanted to prove a point to me by dropping me from the team, and he did also have Thiago back fit again. I would learn later that he always intended to give me a break, so I wouldn't burn out. And this was the perfect time, he just didn't tell me to keep me on my toes. He was a clever man, and a great coach. He always had a plan, even in the difficult days.

We were sitting in a solid mid-table position with the halfway stage of the season approaching. The top two sides were promoted automatically, it looked very much like it was going to be two from Manford, Western Villa and Park Lane United, but the race for the play-offs (the teams who finished 3rd, 4th, 5th and 6th) was wide open. Despite our shocking start, we were only 12 points away from sixth place. With just over half the season still to play, it was still very much game on.

But we could put all that to one side. We had an FA Cup, third round match to prepare for.

"KEEP WORKING HARD, EVEN WHEN NO ONE IS WATCHING." (DEXTER)

The Accies had a great history in the FA Cup. First winning it in 1892 beating Old Corinthians 2-0 in the final. We had won it twelve times since, the third best record, just three wins behind the great Liverton side.

In more recent times, the European challenge had become more important to those in charge of the club. Playing big foreign teams now felt bigger, better and more exciting. As well as giving the club bundles of money every time they played in the main tournaments! The best players wanted to play in it also, so not being in Europe was a big problem when trying to convince the best players from around the world to come. Competing to get into, and then playing in the European cup, or Champions League as it became known, was something the clubs' owners had insisted on every season

Walter in his first few seasons as manager, led the Accies to a semi-final, and the quarter-finals three times in four seasons. But that was now a distant memory, as we stepped out to a stadium that was expecting a five or six goal thumping of the minnows from Middlethian.

I'd always liked the FA cup. I liked the fact that a tiny non-league team of amateur players could play against the best sides about. England internationals verses butchers and traffic wardens. David verses Goliath matches. The big sides nearly always won, but just occasionally there would be a shock, a big one, and now I was praying that the shock result of the round wouldn't be us.

We had been drawn against Middlethian United. A team whose home stadium was right on the border of England and Scotland. We were at home, which helped. But they had nothing to lose and had just seen us thumped 5-0 by Manford. They were an average side at best, even in their own division, and this season they were struggling to win a single match, even down in the fourth tier of English football. It looked to all who watched them that they may well drop into the amateur leagues at the end of this season.

Walter rang the changes after the Manford

demolition, recalling Harry George and Mac into the defence. Monty and Zac were back from their injuries too. Dexter sat this one out for me to return to partner Thiago up front, for the first time. Young Irish defender, Finlay Crane, came in for his debut to replace Arlo who was now suspended for a few games after his sending off. The mood was good, and the players looked relaxed and ready.

We ran out to the usual cheer from the crowd. The chants of 'Wembley, Wembley' were a bit too soon I thought. Every team needs a bit of respect, and to sing a song like this before our first match, in only the third round, in what was the oldest cup competition in the world I thought was a little bit disrespectful, but they were happy and as the sun shone it felt like it was going to be a good day.

We started off really well. The ball zipped around the pitch as we played with pace and confidence. The lower league side had started with five defenders and one of them was intent on hanging onto my shirt at every opportunity.

Still, it didn't seem to matter much, as after only five minutes Zac's arrow like pass found me on the edge of the penalty area. I took it under control with my right foot and hit it first time with my left. It fizzed hard and low and into the corner GOAL! Another cracker. I was made up. That was for Manford, I thought. Wow that felt good.

'Nice one Jack, that was some finish, but the pass was better huh!' Zac joked, winking at me with a massive grin on his face. Middlethian had barely kicked off when J-D hammered into their central midfielder, the ball broke loose to an unmarked Monty who chipped the ball from midway inside their half. The keeper, hopelessly out of position, could only watch as it sailed over his head and into the net.

It was 2-0 and we had only played seven minutes. This is going to be embarrassing for them I thought. I could get bundles of goals today.

But try as we might, the third goal wouldn't come. Some poor shooting, good goalkeeping and brave defending kept the score-line at 2-0 for the rest of the first half. We had our half-time drinks and snacks, relaxed and smiling. Harry G was cracking jokes and even Walter was laughing. No one had any idea what was about to happen.

The second half started in the same way as the first, with us on the attack. Wave after wave, shot after shot. Their goal was living a charmed life and their keeper was certainly going to be

JACK HARVEY

making a name for himself. We had a golden chance to make three-nil when we won a penalty with just 15 minutes left. It was a soft one if I'm honest, a silly foul by their right back, but we didn't mind. It was a chance to make the game totally safe. Thiago stepped up. He had been looking a bit jaded today, after his injury had meant he had not played for a while, but insisted he take it. As the senior striker, we let him, but then wished we hadn't, as after sending the keeper the wrong way, he hit the post. The ball cannoned out straight to a defender who thumped it long and hard. Suddenly they were on the attack and Mac was left in a race with the Middlethian winger. Mac didn't stand a chance as the delighted player burst away before slipping the ball under Lucas. 2-1.

The crowd were silenced, at least for a few moments. We had dominated and were about to put the game to bed, and now – somehow - they were right back in it. I still thought we were more likely to score than them, but Walter decided to make a couple of changes anyway. Thiago who was clearly tiring badly came off, as did Mac who appeared to have pulled a muscle in his desperate foot-chase of the speedy Middlethian winger. But whatever Walter had

63

done had no effect, other than to spur on the away team. There were five minutes to go, and they were the ones playing the ball round like champions. We were chasing shadows. We could feel the tension in the crowd growing and we began to make mistake after mistake. Even Lucas, who was usually so good with his feet, gave the ball away under no pressure, and then as the Middlethian forward pushed the ball back past him, in a desperate attempt to reach the ball, Lucas caught his legs and brought him down. Penalty.

This was NOT happening. We were coasting. This should have been easy. The away fans were bouncing in their little section, and when their star player drilled the penalty kick into the top corner, they exploded with noise. Our supporters were deathly quiet. Somehow, we were going into extra time.

Walter made more changes. He kept me on, but took off both Zac and Monty who had looked totally lost in the last ten minutes. They had quickly become good friends with Lucas and I, and I felt sorry for them, but we needed something to change, and quick.

It didn't work, as whilst we were defensively strong, we couldn't find the killer goal. I was guilty of missing the best chance, blazing the ball over with only seconds of extra time remaining when I really should have at least hit the target.

When the referee blew for full time in extra time, it was a relief. I presumed the game would now go to a replay, but walking back to our huddle on the halfway line I could see Walter scribbling down names.

'Jack, you can have penalty number five, ok?' he barked. He was clearly not happy, but was doing his best to remain calm.

'Penalties? What? Yeah, ok. Sure,' I said. But I wasn't sure. I felt a bit scared of penalty shoot-outs. We had lost our last academy cup final on a penalty shoot-out and whilst I had scored my kick, this was a different matter entirely. This was the FA Cup.

We had won the coin toss and Harry G (who had taken the captaincy for this game from Mac) had decided we were going first.

Finbar was out front and marching towards the spot. Confident walk I thought. He's definitely going to score. He did, no problem, as he calmly slotted it into the bottom corner. They scored 1-1, we scored again through Harry and again as Franco put us 3-2 up. Lucas got a big strong hand to their next one, but was so unlucky as it struck the post, then his shoulder and in, 3-3.

Jamie Curry who had come on as a sub, made it 4-3 before they equalised once again.

It was now my turn. I had expected Lucas to save at least one. He was so good, and he'd hardly had anything to do in the whole game. I walked towards the penalty spot. The goal began to look smaller and smaller, the keeper looked bigger and bigger. I placed the ball on the spot, but the referee insisted I move it more centrally. My hands were shaking as I placed the ball for a second time. I glanced up. The goal looked like a child's training goal and the keeper looked like a giant. I had never been this nervous before.

'Trust yourself' I thought. 'Trust yourself. Laces. Hit it hard with your laces'

Which is what I did. I took a longer than usual run up and smashed the ball straight down the middle, the keeper looked beaten as he dived away to his left, but the ball struck his shins and flew back over my head. I was gutted and could hardly look up as the final Middlethian player walked past me. If he scored, we were out, and it would be a humiliation for the club, and for me.

The competition I loved and respected, was about to give me my most painful memory.

I slumped to the floor as I returned to my teammates on the half-way line. I couldn't look.

Lucas will save it, I prayed, *he always saves one. Please.*

Crack! The sound of the ball hitting the net was the signal for the away team to go crazy. They all charged to pile on top of both their goal-scorer and goalkeeper who would surely be on the back page of every national newspaper tomorrow morning. I trudged off the pitch, got changed - without even having a shower - and ran out of the dressing room without a backward glance. I couldn't face anyone, I just wanted to be alone. I heard Walter coming down the corridor after giving his – very brief - post-match interview. He was bound to be furious, so I dived into one of the storerooms to get away from the anger that I felt surely would be coming my way.

'Don't worry kid,' came a voice. 'No one comes in here. It's just me and the spare kit.' It was Old Billy. So, this is where he hides!

'Billy, I... I messed up,' I said, holding back the tears.

'I saw,' he replied. 'It happens. But if the rest of the team had played better, it would never have reached a shootout. Sometimes even the best players make mistakes. Mistakes when they wish the ground would open up and swallow them.'

'I guess so,' I replied. 'But Walter, he will be so disappointed in me.'

'STOP right there, Jack. There is no way Walt is disappointed in you. Losing the game, yes. But not disappointed in you. You have the talent and desire to take this club back to the top. We can do it this season. But you need to get your head down, and work harder than you ever thought possible. Inspire your mates. The 'Accies kids' as everyone is calling you lot. Monty, Lucas, Zac. They all look up to you. Even Dexter has said you could one day break his scoring records if you stick to it.'

I listened to his every word and began to feel better.

'If you need to sulk to get this out of your system, every time things don't go well, then you won't make it as a pro' he said. 'You need to embrace the defeat. Learn the lessons. How do you feel right now? You make sure that you never feel this way again. Practice, practice, practice. Until you can do it perfectly every single time. Make every skill automatic so you won't even have to think what to do, it will just happen. Watch the game back when you get home and see what you could have done better during the game, then next week put it into action. Dexter still does that after every home game, even after all these years. He comes in here with me and we chat for about an hour, then he takes a copy I have recorded for him, and he goes home to watch it. In fact, I'm sure he'll be here in a minute.'

'Thanks Billy' I said. I was already feeling a lot better, still incredibly disappointed, but knowing that our priority this season was promotion to the Premier League. The FA Cup would have to wait for another season.

'No problem lad,' Billy said. 'I'll see you next week.'

I left his room feeling much better. I was still gutted that we had lost, and I knew the media would not be kind to Walter, the team and probably me too. But I was going to smash training next week and we WERE going to win the next league game.

I lay in bed that night, practicing my deep breathing techniques that always helped me relax. It was something my dad had taught me.

'Whenever things feel a bit much' he would say, 'close your eyes, see what you want to happen. Visualize it, now breathe. Deep breathe. Go out and make it happen.'

I will. I would, and I was going to make it happen, starting tomorrow.

"IT DOES NOT MATTER HOW SLOW YOU THINK YOU ARE GOING, AS LONG AS YOU KEEP GOING AND DON'T STOP." (ZAC)

We were back at it first thing Monday morning. The usual meeting to discuss what had happened in the previous game had been cancelled. There was a darker mood in the air. The coaches moved about quickly and refused to speak to anyone for the first hour or so. We all knew it was going to be a tough day. We were told we were doing double training sessions for the whole week. Session one had started with a fitness test – 'doggies'. As fun as that sounds, doggies involves running between two sets of lines as fast as you can, over and over. Last man back does press-ups, sit-ups, jumping squats etc. Luckily it was not often me. I was still clearly one of the fittest in the first team. But it still hurt and by the time we sat down for our lunch, it felt like I had been running all day.

Lunch was good though. The chef clearly had no hang-ups after our defeat and had piled on the grilled chicken, pesto pasta and avocado. My favourite! After we had eaten, the mood altered slightly. Walter spoke occasionally, but his usual beaming smile was gone. He was angry, and disappointed. That was clear. I don't think he expected us to win the FA Cup, but a decent run would have brought in some money which the club needed to strengthen the squad, and it would have given us confidence to kick on in our quest for promotion.

I was surprised that nothing was really mentioned about the FA Cup defeat. A few passing comments: with, perhaps try this, or possibly try that next time. The word of the day was patience. All the coaches felt that we had been rushing to finish them off and score lots of goals quickly. That impatience we showed meant we had rushed our chances. That, and the fact that their goalkeeper had been incredible. Walter did ask if I was ok later on that week, and like Billy, he just told me to, 'Shrug it off. It happens to everyone sooner or later. Yours was sooner, than you wanted, but next time you will be better prepared.'

He was upset, that was clear. He had taken a lot of stick in the papers and worse still on social media. But there was no doubt in my mind, as well as the other players, that Walter Rolland could restore the club to its rightful place, at the very top of European football. I was desperate to play my part and get us there.

The brief chat with Walter did make me feel a bit better. If missing that penalty had taught me one thing, it was to stay calm and relax, don't rush or force it. I let the situation get the better of me, and whilst I felt a failure, my teammates clearly did not, backing me totally both privately and publicly. Mac even went on TV the next day to do an interview, and what he said totally blew me away:

'Young Jack Harvey has been the highlight of the season for us', he said. 'There was no one else I'd want on that final penalty. Yes, he may have missed his kick, but it should never have reached a shoot-out. We were the better team with better, fitter players. We were more experienced than they were, but we all failed to show that, and we failed to finish the game when we had chance after chance. If you want to put blame on someone then you list the entire team, not just Jack. Young players should be looked after and encouraged, win, lose or draw, and as a team, as a *club, we will all stand with Jack and we will help him recover quickly, because a fit and strong Jack Harvey will win us promotion this season.'*

It was a huge statement and one that really took me back. Mac had always had my back in training and on the pitch during games, he'd made it his job to keep me out of trouble, but to say that publicly made me feel ten feet tall. After hearing what Mac had said I felt great again, and the next day, despite the double session, I was bouncing. I felt fresh and eager to get back into the days' training sessions, no matter how hard they were.

Focus had quickly turned from the Middlethian defeat to the league game against East Athletics. We needed to win to keep the gap to the play-off zone manageable as we approached the halfway point of the season. The training sessions became even more and more intense as the week progressed. Several times Walter had to stop sessions and remind some of the players that we were on the same team, after some rather tasty tackles had been put in!

One thing I had learnt in my short time at Accies was that Walter is a loyal and trusting manager. Other than the return of Mac from injury, he kept faith with the team who had failed to see off Middlethian. This meant I had an immediate chance to set the record straight. We all did. Walter said exactly that in his pre-game press conference.

'Most of these lads underperformed last weekend,' he told the room full of media personnel. 'They know what they need to do to sort it. I trust them that they will do exactly that. As a team we could and should have done much better, but I know that last week was just a blip and I fully expect us to give a good account of ourselves against East.'

And that's exactly what happened. In a perfect response to the last few matches, we scored two goals in each half, Thiago with his first (and second) of the season, another for me and a beauty from the ever-improving Zac, gave us a 4-0 away win. In the next match, Liverford Wanderers put up a bit of a fight, but they were still downed 3-1. Wolfborough, a game which I expected to be very tricky (away in the Wolves Lair as their ground was known), went without incident in a solid 2-0 win. I had scored in each of the last four matches and was delighted with the fact that I was now the club's top-scorer with ten at the halfway point of the season. As a team, we had done well to recover from our shocking start, and stood with ten wins, three draws and six defeats. Sitting on 33 points in tenth place was ok, but nowhere near good enough to get a play-off spot, which usually took 70-75 points.

We needed to up our game considerably.

The next opportunity was when York Town came to the Accies stadium for the first game of the second half of the season. I was able to get revenge for that opening day defeat. Slotting both goals in a comfortable 2-0 win. Goals against Sandford, Heston and Albion followed. With two wins and a draw from those three games, we were now flying up the table and closing in on the sixth place, which would give us a play-off semi-final spot, and maybe even an outside chance of automatic promotion.

The problem was the other teams kept winning too and our first 0-0 draw of the season against Queens Park didn't help. Walter decided to try something a bit more drastic in order to get the goals we really needed

At the Monday meeting it was just us, Walter and the players. No coaches, physios or doctors.

'Is this going to be serious, mate?' I asked Lucas

'Dunno,' he replied. 'Something is up that's for sure.'

'OK Gentleman, listen up,' Walter cried. 'We need to push on hard for promotion. We aren't scoring enough goals and losing silly points to teams we should be smashing off the pitch is going to hurt us at the end of the season. We need to utilise our strengths. We are going to dominate the ball, in their half by playing our three best forwards all at once. We will be relying on the midfielders to increase their work rate, but I think we have the fittest boys in the country. This is the team selection for Saturday,' he said unveiling the team he had scribbled on the touch screen.

Three up front? It was bold. I was excited. I'd played (briefly) with both Dex and Thiago, but never at the same time. This new look side looked like it could score goals from everywhere. And so it proved as we smashed both Wealdmore and Workington 4-0, Oxfield 3-1 and East Cove 5-2 in a pulsating game. My goals tally was shooting up, only behind the main men at both Western Villa and Manford in the race for the golden boot, (which was the award given to the league's top goal-scorer).

We were now on a great run, unbeaten since the FA Cup defeat, but back-to-back draws hindered us once again in our charge up the table. Not for lack of trying, it was more that the goalkeepers enjoyed playing against such a big team and played their best game of the season. It was frustrating for us, but also strangely satisfying in a way. Despite our position, the other teams saw us as the best side in the league and treated us as such. But even with these minor setbacks, we were still right in the hunt in what was becoming one of the most competitive play-off races for years. We scrapped away to get the three points in our next game before a big week when we played the top two sides back-to-back.

Western Villa was first up, and as before it was a terrific game. Lots of good football played by both sides. Villa were desperate to close the gap on Manford (who were beginning to pull away at the top of the table), but Lucas was having a great game. They did eventually beat him late on, but almost from the restart Fin hit a worldie of a pass right to my feet and I curled a beauty into the top corner for 1-1 as we salvaged a draw.

We had six games to go. I'd worked out to be sure we needed to win five of them, maybe only four if we were really lucky. Beating old Wimbledonians away from home was a good start, but next up was the mighty Manford. Away.

There could be no doubt, it would be a battle.

"IF YOU ARE ALONE, JACK, YOU CAN ONLY DO SO MUCH. TOGETHER WE WILL MOVE MOUNTAINS." (LUCAS)

Manford Rovers were closing in on the championship title. They needed one more win to be assured of promotion and first position seemed to be a nailed-on certainty. Judging by what they were saying pre-game, they were fully intent to finish the job against us. We had a full-strength side to choose from once again, but they had their big two forwards who had haunted us in the first game back, one from injury and the other having served a suspension for a red card in a previous game.

They looked formidable and there was little doubt in my mind that they would regain their place in the Premier League. But despite the setbacks of a few draws in the league, we were unbeaten for 18 matches. It would be a great game. We hadn't lost a league game since the thrashing Manford gave us at the Accies stadium. But away from home, well this was another huge test. Manford not only had the best home record in the division, but it was also the best home record in the whole of the UK. This would be their 22nd home match in all competitions, and so far, they had won 20 and drawn only one. They were still in the FA Cup having beaten two Premier League sides so far. Beating them would be a formidable task. We were only two points behind sixth place Wolfborough, but a defeat could spell the end of our charge to the end of season play-offs.

We were all optimistic; Mac was his usual excitable self, Walter was super-positive and running out I felt that it would time for revenge. It was not to be the case. In fact, after 25 minutes of the match I couldn't see anything other than another heavy defeat. In a near carbon copy of the first match against them, we were two goals and a man down, and struggling to hold on to the mighty Manford strikers. Dexter had seen a very early red card for a rash challenge. One he later admitted was reckless and stupid. But as the half drew to a close, instead of falling apart, we began to play some really good football. Something inside me clicked, it felt good, it felt so much better! I couldn't understand or explain quite how I felt like this, but I did. I believed in my team; I believed in Walter and his advice. But best of all, I really believed in myself: I could make a difference, I knew I could make the change we needed to get back into this match.

'Lads,' Walter barked, 'we are still in this. They have given us their everything, and they know we will not go away. We need to pressure them higher and higher, force them into mistakes. No one has dared go for them the way that we will in this second half. They won't like it and they won't know how to deal with it.'

It was a stirring speech and it got us going. The second half started and we exploded into life. Almost immediately, Monty was down the wing, crossing for me at the back post, but just as I was about to strike the ball the Manford keeper and I crashed into each other, and I was sent tumbling end over end. All I could hear was shouting and the referee's whistle. I lay face down waiting for the cheers for what I thought would be my red card, but in fact it was the other way. Their keeper had hit me far too early and was given his marching orders. We were ten men each, but they had lost their keeper and their substitute goalie was young, untried and untested.

His first job was to pick the ball out of the net

as Thiago smashed the penalty into the top right corner. Our tails were up, and we went time and again at Manford. To his credit, and despite his obvious nerves, their replacement keeper did quite well. It was his long heavy clearance that set up a chance for their killer striker, who slotted past Lucas, 1-3. Totally against the run of play. But despite this huge setback we knew we were the better side, we knew we would have more chances the way we were playing.

Having received the ball from Zac after one of his typically bone-crunching tackles, I played a quick one-two with Monty before thumping the ball goal-wards. It caught the keepers' right hand and looked to be heading out for a corner, but there, flying in at the back post was Thiago, and he was able to slide it home, 2-3 and it really was game on now with ten minutes left.

We pushed hard, we pressed high. The Manford players were out on their feet with exhaustion, but we kept on going and going. Closing in on injury time, I pleaded with Fin and Zac to get me the ball.

'Just get it to me, anywhere, any way you can. The guy who is marking me can't keep up with me. He's dead on his feet, just give me one chance,' I begged.

Then, Lucas found Arlo with one of his arrow

like throws. Arlo's curling pass down the line found Monty. He tucked it inside to Fin who pinged it first time to my feet. I controlled it instantly, turned and ran at full speed towards my marker. He swung a tired leg, catching my trailing foot, but even though I was stumbling I kept going. Away and free, just the substitute keeper to beat, I could see Zac steaming up on my left, but so did the keeper, and the second he looked to see what Zac was doing I pushed the ball to my right, rounded him and rolled the ball into an empty net. 3-3! We had done it. Against the odds we had come back, and whilst it was only one point gained, it felt like a win. Doubly so, when we found that the only other side who could realistically pip us to sixth place, Wolfborough, had also only been able to draw their match, maintaining the gap between the two teams, to only two points.

We were elated, and I felt brilliant. The media said that my goal was the best they had seen at the Manford stadium all season, and there had been a lot of goals there! The Manford players were furious with the result, but on TV their captain said that although they had scored three goals, he felt fortunate to have not lost their unbeaten record.

'That was the hardest game we have had all

season, including against the two Premier League clubs,' he stated. 'If Accies had started the season like that, today's game would have been the championship decider for sure.'

It was thrilling for me to hear that, and we all took a massive confidence boost from it. We carried on our fine form beating Landon Borough, East Athletics and Liverford but so did our closest rivals, meaning it was a winner take all match against Wolfborough, at home to decide who would make the play-offs.

I was excited. It was my first real taste of what a senior cup final might feel like. Win and we were into the end-of-season four team play-off; lose and the season was over right then and there.

'How are you feeling mate?' It was Lucas. He looked slightly anxious, well, he looked more worried than usual. Lucas didn't really do *worried*.

'I'm ok, I'm excited. It's going to be a big game' I replied. 'How are you feeling mate?'

'I'm fine Jack,' Lucas replied. 'We've come so far this season. Do you really think we can do this?'

'Yes,' I said, 'I totally trust you, and all the lads. We've been magnificent. I just hope I can live up to everyone's expectations' I told him.

'Just treat it like any other game, ok?' he said. 'We've got this.'

I knew he was right. We had Dex back in the squad after his three-match suspension and we all felt good. Even if Dex's career was all but over, whatever happened next he was still a legend on and off the pitch. We all loved him and loved having him around. He always knew the right thing to say and when to say it. Whilst Thiago was the better player now, Dex was still my favourite to play with. He and Mac had been my mentors through the season; Mac with his noisy encouragement, and Dex leading by example on and off the pitch.

I could not have asked for any better.

Wolfborough were a good team, we knew that, but we knew we were better. We just had to show it, prove it to them, to the supporters, and the TV stations who had picked up the match to broadcast live. We started like men possessed, attacking at every opportunity, down the left, down the right, balls over the top. After 30 minutes I could see a couple of the Wolves' players were taking a knee. Stealing extra seconds at the restarts, just to catch their breath. We were relentless, wave after wave of blue and yellow shirts poured forward. It was like we had two or three extra players at times, and when Dex rattled the post, the ball rebounded kindly to Thiago who smashed it into the roof of the unguarded net 1-0.

BOOM! We were on our way. But no one was happy to settle for just one. We went for them again and again. A second goal followed from a lovely strike from Dex, picking up my carefully threaded pass before finding the bottom corner, and early in the second half I managed to scuff home Fin's cross-come-shot for 3-0. Wolfborough just couldn't get going. We didn't let them, Lucas hardly had a save to make, certainly nothing difficult. We were in the play-offs. One game away from Wembley, and just two wins for an immediate and unlikely return to the Premier league.

We were drawn against Newford Celtic, and as we had finished sixth and last of the four teams, we would be away from home for the semi-final.

'Ok chaps,' Walter boomed out after the Wolves game, 'We've done the easy bit, we've got to the business end of the season, and we are still in with a chance. A big chance. I do not want to finish empty handed. We will go out and flatten this Celtic side. We've beaten them away already this season and we can do it again. I believe in you, we all do. Take the opportunity, they won't give it to you. YOU have to take it,' he said as he pointed around his head to the blue and yellow wall of noise that was bouncing and singing our names.

'Do it for them, do it for us, but most of all, do it for yourselves. Never, ever quit!'

I wished the game was right now. I was ready to play another 90 minutes straight away. I felt great. I felt good. I couldn't stop scoring goals. I was bubbling over with excitement.

One win and we are at Wembley, I thought. It was so close I could virtually touch it.

"TALENT MAY WIN US A FEW GAMES, BUT TEAMWORK AND HARD WORK WILL WIN US TROPHIES." (MAC)

We went into the semi-final on one of the best unbeaten runs in the club's history. We hadn't lost in the last 22 games, (24 if you include the Middlethian cup game which technically was a draw). We had scored buckets of goals, and despite Thiago missing a large chunk of the season he was on 20 goals. I, quite incredibly, and to me, unbelievably, was the club's top scorer on 24 goals. I would become the youngest Accies player ever to reach 25 should I bag one more, but this would be a massive bonus.

We were all totally focused on the job in hand.

Mac as usual was barking at everyone.
'Never give up, never quit. Run till your legs come off! Don't stop. If it hurts you, it hurts them more.'

As the club captain, Mac took his role as motivator very seriously. The younger lads, Fin, Zac, Monty and Lucas, were still utterly terrified of him, but now I knew him better than they did, and under his fierce front he was kind and generous. (As a present after our final league match, he'd bought me a new pair of trainers, expensive ones!).

'Jacko,' he boomed 'I've felt bad since I ruined your last ones. Have these! I promise not to steal the laces this time. You've been a superstar for us this season.'

'Thanks Mac,' I replied. 'And I promise not to nutmeg you again. At least, not more than once a day!'

We both grinned. We were in the best frame of mind possible, and on a warm Wednesday evening at the Newford Celtic stadium, we played like we had wings on our backs and jet boosters in our heels.

The first half though was evenly contested, a couple of chances each, with both keepers doing enough to keep it scoreless. But we had the better of the possession. We were moving the ball with purpose, and much faster than they were. We were running harder and were clearly more committed. We looked like a much stronger team going into the half-time interval.

Our style of play was aggressive and constant. The other teams were chasing shadows and using up all their energy just to stay in the game. Sooner or later, they would make a mistake. I was sure that it was going to happen today, and soon. And so, I was proved right.

Zac and Fin had chased the Celtic full-back into the corner, and his sliced clearance landed in front of a charging Thiago, who, after controlling the ball on his chest, volleyed an unstoppable rocket past the Newford keeper for 1-0. When Mac's thumping header from a corner made it 2-0 the game was all but over. The Newford players had been dragged all over the pitch and had nothing left to give. We saw out the last 15 minutes easily, even adding one more as Zac burst through on one of his typically surging runs to make it 3-0.

We were off to Wembley and the play-off final. One game away from a return to what I thought was the best division in the world.

We would face Park Lane United. They had seen off Sanford Warriors in the other semi-final easily. They had been very disappointed not to win automatic promotion, and were easily the favourites to win and go up, despite the form we were in. Park had spent a lot of money in the summer and were on a mission to get back to the Premier League. They had the best young players outside of the top division, as well as some very good senior players who were too good not to be in the Premier League. We were the underdogs for sure, and they let us know it. Their manager telling anyone who would listen that they were much better than us, and they would win, and win comfortably.

Walter didn't like this. He didn't like it at all.

'I do not want to start a war of words,' he told the media. We could tell he was boiling underneath, but he kept his emotions in check – just! He continued, 'I prefer to let my team do the talking. He thinks his team is good, and I agree with him. They are. But we have a very good team also. Let's just see who does the talking on Saturday evening, after the match.'

Our team was again unchanged for the final, which was great as we knew each other's game so well now. As we trooped out in a long line, we could see that most of the stadium was blue and yellow. Our fans were the best, well, I've always thought so. When I was younger, I learnt quickly that when a team came to our home stadium and beat us, it was a big deal, but that we had to stay and applaud them off the pitch.

'It's called being humble son,' my dad had told me. 'We celebrate when we win, and we do usually win here, a lot. But when we lose, we applaud our team for trying and doing their best, but we also let the other team know who we are and what we believe in, by letting them know that we appreciate their efforts, because it won't happen again!'

I looked over the hordes of Accies supporters; there was a pure white section at the far end, matching the gleaming white kit of the Park players. I had to admit they looked the business, but when they looked over at us, they saw Mac. I know who I'd be more frightened of!

Park kicked off to a huge roar. 90,000 fans. It felt like 90 million fans, the noise was unlike anything I'd ever heard. We had to scream to each other to be heard, and even then, it was next to impossible.

The first ten minutes flew by. Thiago, Dex and I had hardly had a kick as we struggled to get into the game. After 20 minutes, Zac, Arlo, Alfie and Dex had all picked up yellow cards, as well as three of the Park players. It was 100mph and many of the tackles were just not fast enough to keep up. We tried to play our usual game, but at that speed the passes just weren't there.

It would need a moment of luck to get on top, or one of incredible skill. Luckily, we got a big

chunk of both. Park had won a corner. As I trotted back to take up my usual position on the edge of the box, where I would lurk, hoping that I could grab any loose passes and run the ball to safety, Mac bellowed to me,
'Jacky, Jack lad, stay up.'

I looked at him quizzically. I had done this ever since I broke into the team. This would be a first. And in such an important game? I shrugged at Mac and carried on walking back.

'No' he shouted, 'get up, halfway line!'

Dex was already there, but I could see Mac's logic. With two of us upfield, and with my pace, it prevented one of Park's big defenders from coming up to attack the corner, making it easier for our defenders to mark their players. It didn't seem to work though, as we couldn't stop them breaking through our defensive line. A towering header from the other giant central defender was whistling to the top corner, until a huge, gloved hand came from nowhere and turned the header onto the underside of the bar and out. The rebound fell perfectly for the Park forward who hammered it goal-wards, but somehow the falling Lucas managed to extend his legs, the ball struck his shin and cannoned up the pitch. It was an extraordinary double save.

The rebound fell to Dex, who quick as a flash had turned his marker and was looking up, looking for me! He may have lost his speed, but his mind was still super-fast, so without really thinking I set off, and Dex, using all his years of experience, hit a lovely ball into the space. I knew no one could catch me in a 50-50, let alone with a head start, and I powered down on goal. The keeper came out, narrowing the angle, to try and make it harder for me, but I was going so fast it felt easy to just glide past him and as I fell sideways, I was able to guide the ball into the empty net. It was a glorious goal, and one that deserved to take us to the promised land of the Premier League.

But Park themselves had determination in them and refused to lie down. They laid siege to our goal and time and time again our young team had to put our bodies on the line. The old guard, Mac, Dex and Arlo, led by example, running their hearts out and by half time, still leading 1-0, I was beginning to get concerned. Dex already looked spent, and Mac was struggling to hang onto his younger and more pacy forward.

'We keep going'! Walter boomed. He was pacing up and down the dressing room, almost bouncing off the walls. I loved his energy. He was always (well nearly always) smiling. He loved his players, and we all loved him. We really would run through walls for him.

'Jack, a word please,' he said.

We walked into a smaller side room. I was concerned that I was going to be removed in a tactical switch; it was the opposite.

'Dex has nearly checked out,' he said. 'He's already close to exhaustion. I'm going to give him another ten minutes then he's off. You will be up top on your own, with Thiago behind you. You run them off the pitch, ok? Can you do that for me?'

He gave me a huge smile and a wink.

'Of course, boss, of course I can. Just give me the ball!'

He laughed and returned to the dressing room.

We ran out in the second half, to the same onslaught as the first half. I couldn't quite believe we were still 1-0 up, they were so good, and so fast. We couldn't cope with their power and pace. But there, like a rock at the back, time and time again, was my best mate, Lucas Cain. He was a human wall. His double save in the first half was extraordinary, but his performance so far was incredible. He caught everything, saved everything, until 15 minutes from the end: disaster struck.

A long Park cross sailed into our penalty area. One of the Park Lane forwards was running onto it, more in hope more than belief. Lucas came out to collect it, rising easily into the air clutching it into his chest, but as he fell, he landed on the Park forward. Lucas' ankle rolled horribly as he landed back on the pitch, and he fell to the ground in awful pain. As he went down the ball broke loose, and it was a simple task for the Park player to roll it in, 1-1.

It was obvious that Lucas stood no chance of carrying on, and he had to be substituted for our reserve keeper Jordan James. JJ, as we all called him, had not had a chance in the first team yet, this would be his debut. He looked terrified as he ran onto the pitch, gloveless! Walter hurriedly called him back to collect his gloves and carry on. The Park players smelt blood and immediately peppered him with crosses. Whilst before, Lucas had claimed everything, JJ stayed nervously on his line, shouting: 'Away, head it away!' at every opportunity. It was only a matter of time it seemed, and true enough Park soon scored their second. A cross was headed away by Zac, but only to the edge of the box and bang, a rocket of a shot whistled under the body of the helpless JJ and into the net 1-2.

Zac looked at JJ. He wasn't impressed, clearly feeling that JJ should have done better.

'I can't believe it, we've come so far, and now this?' Zac said, looking downcast.

'Zac,' I said, 'it's not over. Get me the ball, anyway you can, just get me the ball. I still believe. Anything is possible. Just believe in yourself. Believe in me.'

'Ok mate.' Zac said. 'Let's do this'. He clapped his hands and let out a roar of 'COME OOOOON!' facing up to the main stand where the support was 100% blue and yellow. The crowd sensed it and increased the noise. It was unlike anything I had ever experienced before. The hair on the back of my neck stood up.

We kicked off and knew that we only had a couple of minutes to save the season. To lose now, after the run we had been on, would have been heartbreaking. But we were going to try. The fans were doing all they could to spur us on. Monty, who was possibly playing his last game for us, as his loan was due up after this game, won the ball on the halfway line. He found Fin on his inside who quickly switched the play to Zac who was now on the wing. As soon as he got the ball, I knew we were on. I motored down the centre as Zac ducked and weaved past a couple of tiring Park defenders before curling a brilliant cross that just eluded the keeper, but not me. I slid across the pitch, catching the ball on the volley with my outstretched leg and screamed with delight as the ball hit the back of the net.

2-2.

The crowd went crazy. 90 seconds left, and we had equalised. I was mobbed by my team-mates, but the game wasn't yet over. Park would surely come back strong in extra time. But before then, we had to hold out until the final whistle was blown.

We did more than that.

Gianfranco Spaletti who had come on earlier for Dex - and until now had done nothing other than give away the ball, or concede silly free kicks - decided he was going to show us some of his famed Italian magic. He won the ball back on the edge of our area, before setting off down the left. There seemed no real danger, and he had been so poor since coming on the Park players didn't look bothered in trying to get the ball back, expecting that true to form he would give the ball back to them. But, without warning, he hit overdrive and burst past two stationary Park players, jinking right, swerving left. He had beaten five players before rolling the ball inside to Thiago. Thiago drew his leg back to shoot, and just as he was about to pull the trigger, he was taken out by a desperate Park defender. PENALTY!

It was well into injury time; it was 2-2 in the play-off final.

We had a penalty.

Thiago, he wouldn't miss, would he? But Thiago wasn't getting up. The Park player had hammered into him, and he was clearly in a lot of pain, struggling to stand. I looked around. Who else was going to take it? Arlo? Fin?

'Jack,' Thiago called. 'It's your time. You take it. Be the hero today.'

'But Thiago, after last time,' I tried to change his mind.

'No last time Jack, forget what happened last time. See the ball hit the net. Use the lessons you've learnt. You can do this,' he grinned. 'Do it for us. Do it for them,' he smiled, looking up at the fans.

I reluctantly picked up the ball and walked into the penalty area. I glanced up at the Park keeper who was stood on the edge of his six-yard box, refusing to move. He looked huge. The referee insisted he step back, and he eventually did, but only after collecting a yellow card. He was bouncing about, punching the cross-bar, doing everything he could to distract me.

I closed my eyes. I took a deep breath, thought of my mum and dad sat in one of the family areas, thought of Izzy - no doubt leading the cheering in the stands, telling anyone who would listen that I was her brother, and that she and I would one day both play for the mighty Accies. I imagined the ball hitting the net, and in that moment, I remembered what old Billy had told me at the end of last season.

You are the future of this club. You will bring it back to greatness, but you must believe in yourself'

He was right, I could, I would, and I will.

I started my run up, head down running faster and faster. I reached the ball and drilled it hard and low towards the bottom right corner. The keeper guessed right and had moved early. His fingers grasped at the ball. The ball clipped the inside of the post, and it was in. It went IN!

3-2 Accies!

I'd scored a hat trick in the play-off final, at Wembley, the national stadium and I wasn't even aware that I had! I was buried under a sea of blue and yellow shirts. The referee didn't even bother to kick off, and blew the final whistle. That's it, we've won! We have been promoted. From a seemingly desperate situation we had fought back, through adversity I was the hero! Everyone was running about like crazy. Even Lucas was hopping over and joined the pile of delighted players.

We had lived our dream. I had conquered my fears, and by scoring the penalty I had put my face in every newspaper and on every sports media channel across the country. I didn't care though; it was a dream come true.

My beloved Accies were going back to the Premier League, and next season I would be able to match myself up against some of the best players in the world.

FINAL TABLE

	TEAM	P	W	D	L	GF	GA	PTS
1	MANFORD ROVERS	38	31	8	1	112	26	101
2	WESTERN VILLA	38	28	6	4	98	36	90
3	PARK LANE UNITED	38	27	5	6	93	42	86
4	NEWFORD CELTIC	38	26	6	5	87	41	84
5	SANFORD WARRIORS	38	24	10	4	87	41	82
6	ACCIES	38	24	8	6	82	39	80
7	WOLFBOROUGH	38	23	10	6	78	42	79

☐ CHAMPIONS ▨ PROMOTED

103

SEASON RESULTS 2:0

TEAM	HOME/AWAY	GOALS FOR	GOALS AGAINST	SCORERS
YORKTOWN	AWAY	0	2	
SANFORD WARRIORS	HOME	0	1	
HESTON BULLS	HOME	1	1	Brooks
ALBION ADMIRALS	AWAY	2	3	Spaletti 2
QUEENS PARK	HOME	1	1	Brooks
WEALDMORE FALCONS	AWAY	0	3	
WOKINGTON	HOME	1	3	Brooks
WESTERN VILLA	AWAY	2	1	Brooks, Harvey
EAST COVE	HOME	3	0	Harvey 2, Brooks
NEWFORD CELTIC	AWAY	4	1	Montgomery, Smith, Bernard, MacRandall
PARK LANE UNITED	AWAY	3	1	Brooks 2, Montgomery
ARLINGTON COUNTY	HOME	2	0	Harvey 2
OXFIELD CITY	AWAY	1	0	Harvey
OLD WIMBLEDONIANS	HOME	3	0	Brooks 3
MANFORD ROVERS	HOME	0	5	
LANDON BOROUGH	AWAY	1	1	Talbot
MIDDLETHIAN UNITED	HOME	2 (4pens)	2 (5pens)	Harvey, Montgomery
EAST ATHLETICS	AWAY	4	0	Felipe 2, Montgomery, Smith
LIVERFORD WANDERERS	HOME	3	1	Harvey, Montgomery, Felipe

WOLFBOROUGH	AWAY	2	0	Harvey, Felipe
YORK TOWN	HOME	2	0	Harvey 2
SANFORD WARRIORS	AWAY	3	0	Harvey, Felipe, Montgomery
HESTON BULLS	AWAY	4	1	Harvey, MacRendall, Talbot 2
ALBION ADMIRALS	HOME	2	0	Harvey, Felipe
QUEENS PARK	AWAY	0	0	
WEALDMORE FALCONS	HOME	4	0	Harvey, Felipe 2, Smith
WOKINGTON	AWAY	4	0	Talbot, Felipe, Brooks, Spaletti
OXFIELD CITY	HOME	3	1	George, Talbot, Brooks
EAST COVE	AWAY	5	2	Harvey 2, Montgomery, Felipe
NEWFORD CELTIC	HOME	2	2	Felipe 2
PARK LANE UNITED	HOME	1	1	Montgomery
ARLINGTON COUNTY	AWAY	1	0	Brooks
WESTERN VILLA	HOME	1	1	Harvey
OLD WIMBLEDONIANS	AWAY	3	1	Harvey, Felipe, Bernard
MANFORD ROVERS	AWAY	3	3	Felipe 2, Harvey
LANDON BOROUGH	HOME	3	1	Felipe 3
EAST ATHLETICS	HOME	2	0	Felipe, Harvey
LIVERFORD WANDERERS	AWAY	3	2	MacRendall, Talbot, Harvey
WOLFBOROUGH	HOME	3	0	Felipe, Brooks, Harvey
NEWFORD CELTIC	AWAY	3	0	Felipe, MacRendall, Smith
PARK LANE UNITED	WEMBLEY	3	2	Harvey 3

ABOUT THE AUTHOR

James Hewlett was born and raised on the Channel Island of Jersey. Surrounded by the sea and lush, green fields, his passion was sports: playing, watching, and dreaming of being a famous footballer like his hero, 'Roy of the Rovers'.

Father to Harvey and Robyn, he began sports writing in 2008 for local papers, magazines and the Jersey Reds Rugby Club, where he still volunteers both as a junior coach and as part of the media team.

'Breakthrough' is his first book in a series of fast-paced, feel-good football action-adventure stories, telling the career of local boy Jack Harvey, and the Accies - his boyhood team.